A hidden village lies just beneath the clouds, above the valley on top of mineral rich mountains. Tiny ambers fly across the hills from a nearby wildfire. Strange flames spark a tale of an African American cowboy's legacy. Arriving in the early 1850's as runaway slaves, Stanley & Wilkens found a village on the top of an obscure mountain range. High above sea level on the flat mountaintops rest thousands of acres. Many slaves escaped to the north. Some were lucky enough to never get caught, and others were even luckier to make it to secret Grandmother Land. This place held special roots. An ancient land in the clouds full of rivers, streams, lakes, forest and jungles. From fields, to dunes, trees, cacti, cabins and igloos; this place had everything. It was the closest to the moon. Copper skin Aboriginal Indians were the first settlers here before the

Transatlantic and Indigenous slave trades. Grandmother land provided everything for man. It was left vacant for nearly 250 years until Stanley & Wilkens escaped the chains of captivity. They stole a five horse pulled wagon and managed to get their entire families to freedom. Both families were generations of hard working men and even stronger women who soon founded the County of Hollow Hills.

Welcome to Hollow Hills

Da Kozmoz Publishing Presents

"Wildfire"

Natural Disaster Series
Vol.1
(Grandmother Land)

Written by
Gravity G. Pull /Judeau Da Planet

Table of Contents

Introduction. Page 1

Title page 3

Copyrights page 4

Table of Contents page 5

Chapter 1 (6/19/1855) "Young Albert Stanley" .page 7

Chapter 2 "Mr.Albert Stanley Sr, in the year 1905" . page 17

Chapter 3 (1910) "Sage; a Different Name for a Different Girl" . page 23

Chapter 4 (1911)"The County of Hollow Hills Inmate" . page 30

Chapter 5 (The Early 1870s)"Furious Family Feud" . page 35

Chapter 6 (1916) "Pure Prime Beef" .page 41

Chapter 7 (1885) "Murphy O'Connor, escape to the states" . page 49

Chapter 8 (1899-1916) "Malcolm, Grace & Nathan" . page 53

Chapter 9 "The Late 1920's Irish meeting" page 60

Chapter 10 (1929) Phase Two Irish Revenge" page 65

Chapter 1
"Young Albert Stanley"

Young Albert Stanley grew up on a small ranch in the late 1800's raising cattle with his father, William Stanley Jr and grandfather William Stanley Sr. The Stanley ranch was a family business that flourished and expanded with his family's hard work, dedication, blood, sweat and tears.

A few decades after slavery was abolished, Al turned twelve years old on Juneteenth 1885. Young Albert and his dog Cody ventured over the property line, running through vacant fields and onto the old Wilkens farm. Little Al enjoyed skipping through the cornfield chasing Cody. Out of nowhere, he tripped over a leg sticking out of the corn maze. He got up, brushed his face off and saw Mr.Wilkens foot sticking out a pile of clovers. Al ran to tell his grandfather what he just saw.

Al said, "Grandfather you must come quick, it's Mr.Wilkens, He is covered in clovers!"

Giant balls of clovers blew in the wind like tumbleweeds as the paramedics arrived. Al took Cody inside. He couldn't believe what just happened.

A month later his grandfather William Stanley Sr purchased the old Wilkens farm and expanded the Stanley ranch across the property line. The old Wilkens farm was special to Al because it had a wooden tower on it that Mr.Wilkens used for a water reserve. During droughts he had enough water to share with neighbors, water his crops, clean his tractors and drink all summer long with that old wooden tower. The Wilkens farm also had a plethora of crops Al could enjoy with Cody.

One day, after a few years passed when Al was fifteen, he woke up to find his grandfather standing in the kitchen with a bottle of molasses yelling, "The wildfire will spin for years to come! Beware we are no longer safe in Hollow Hills! The world will burn for the next two hundred years!"

He grabbed his chest and fell to the floor. As the molasses bottle shattered across the kitchen floor in slow motion. The room started spinning and everything got blurry. Al hurried up and dialed nine one one and the paramedics took his grandfather away on a gurney. He suffered a minor heart attack.

The coming wildfire season was too much for him to handle. It was unusual and very rare for wildfires to reach the county of Hollow Hills; but before the Doctors loaded grandfather into the medical helicopter, William Stanley Sr predicted a global wildfire would spread like a flaming hurricane on Jupiter.

Al got in the helicopter with him and they flew him to the hospital across the street from the hotel. As the helicopter flew higher, Al could see the hidden city above the clouds like he never did before. Al never realized how important his ranch was until that day. Then it happened; Al saw a vision as he held his grandfather's hand in the helicopter.

Al said, "Grandfather, I know how to save the ranch."

His grandfather couldn't reply with an oxygen mask on his face, but he saw the vision as Al explained the details. Tears ran down his grandfather's cheek as he held Al's hand. He saw the same vision Al did. He pulled his hands back and aimed an invisible rifle. The invisible shot rang off; bang! Splash! Al saw grandfather's smile beneath the mask and prepared to run to the hotel as soon as the helicopter landed.

The wildfire hurricane was now only one-hundred miles south and ready to fly away, moving toward the Hills and ready to climb the rich vegetation.

During grandfather's ride, Al called his father William Stanley Jr and said, "Grandpa's instinct was right. The wildfire was moving fast, consuming everything in its path. I can see the hurricane of flames from the helicopter. You must get everyone out-of-town now before it's too late!"

All the Stanley's started packing for the hotel, as the mayor and fire chief began evacuating all citizens. The sheriff began preparing for a full-blown wildfire war. Al's family quickly finished packing and left to stay in a hotel across the street from the hospital grandpa was in.

Young Al insisted he go back with his father to prepare the ranch. With grandfather sick, he knew the day ahead would be tough. He helped his father set up generators to keep sprinklers running. He sprayed retardant and loaded up the cattle into the trailers.

About a day had passed since they transported grandfather Stanley to the hospital. A local news update played across the radio, and the local authorities continued to order mandatory evacuations for the first time in the county's history. The wildfire was less than fifty miles away and already burned five hundred and fifty acres below the valley. Growing stronger by the minute, moving even faster than seven miles per hour.

Young Al looked at his father and froze as the smoke poured into his view. It was time to go. Nothing else they could do but haul the cattle away to a safer place. Time came to be with the family.

It was one thing that bothered young Al the most. Several generations of the Stanley family worked this land their entire life. This was his roots; ancient ancestors carved this village that his grandfather ran. He couldn't give up that easily.

He remembered his vision and put it into action. With his father William Jr stuck in disarray, young Al stashed grandfather's rifle in the truck. They quickly headed to the hotel. Young Al was determined to go through with his vision. He knew no one would let him go, so he didn't tell anyone what he was planning. While everyone was crying and trying to keep things together at the hotel, he pondered the vision.

Young Al waited until the very late hours of the night somewhere between dusk and dawn before anyone had awoken to put his plan in effect. He stole the family truck, put it in neutral so no one could hear it and steered it down the road, then started it up in second gear, speeding on a trailblazing highway to help. He headed straight back to the ranch.

Young Al pulled over with the Wilkens old wooden water tower in his sight, grabbed the rifle out of the truck and shot as many holes into the tower as he could.

It was like a giant beach pale spilling over, flooding the nearby lot and wetting the grounds rich like a marshland. He created a moat around several acres of land. The creek flooded, pushing the wildfire around the Stanley ranch as it slowly faded away. The water ran down the hills, putting out the hurricane of flames.

Meanwhile, back at the hotel, William Jr got a phone call. The nurse said, "Grandpa is having some major difficulties. Come over!"

At that very moment, the family realized young Al was missing. They rushed across the street to the hospital and to their surprise Al was holding grandpa's hand.
William Jr yelled at Al, "Why did you leave? Where is my truck?"

With his last breath William Sr said, "Oh don't worry son, young Al saved the Stanley ranch. Our vision came true. I am very proud of him and you should be too!"

William Stanley Sr squeezed Al's hand
and smiled one last time.

Chapter 2
"Mr.Albert Stanley Sr in the year 1905"

Seventeen years passed since Al's grandfather William Stanley Sr predicted the wildfire hurricane that came up to the clouds like a scared mountain goat. Young Al wasn't young anymore; he grew up to become Mr.Albert Stanley Sr; also known as Al Sr. He had a family of his own now. A lovely wife Mrs.Albert Stanley and two beautiful twins Albert Jr and Alberta.

Al Sr and his father William Jr kept the family legacy going strong. Expanding a few acres each year by purchasing some land that burned in the wildfire hurricane twenty years ago. Even though the mountains weren't as rich in minerals anymore, the Stanley's tried to support more herds, so they continued to purchase whatever was available and affordable. They connected several lots to their land up and down the hills.

Over the years, Al Sr and his father tried their best to revitalize the land they purchased. Unfortunately, they weren't very successful. Al's mother was much older now and thinking of moving to a small cabin nearby. She wanted to get away from the daily chores and hard work in the kitchen. The Stanley's household didn't have enough money for Al's Mr. & Mrs.William Stanley to retire yet.

One Sunday morning, William Jr got up an hour earlier than usual and headed out to the pastures to start work. As he loaded up the pickup truck with gear, he had an evil idea. William Jr continued on, but it was a change in his plans.

He gathered the gasoline cans, leaving the generators behind. He drove to the edge of the mountaintop, then turned the truck off. Grabbing two gasoline cans out of the truck, he ran into the small forest that grew down the mountainside. William Jr made sure he was well across the property line before he began to pour the gasoline all over the brush and greenery.

Mr.Albert Stanley Sr got up and headed out on his daily routine and noticed the truck and gear missing but the generators were still covered under the tarps.

He said to himself, "Something is fishy; dad would never leave the generators!"

So he grabbed his hunting rifle and followed the tire tracks that led to footprints into the small forest beyond the cliff boundary. The stink of gasoline lingered in the morning air. Al Sr ran over to his truck the thief left at the edge of the property line. He quickly used the truck's radio to alert the authorities. Then it happened. Out of the morning dew mixed with gasoline fumes, William Jr jumped on top of the truck with a cigar and a lighter.

Al Sr yelled, "Father, no! It will blow!"

William Jr smiled and said, "The home insurance will pay for everything five times over the value, son."

Al Sr yelled, "No, father! I can't let you do this, it's grandfather's legacy! We can't give up. Do you remember The Great Baltimore Fire of 1904?"

Al Sr pointed the rifle at William Jr and shouted, "Put the lighter down now, or I will shoot you!"

William Jr replied, "Shoot me! I do recall what happened in Baltimore, but I'd rather die before I work another day in these hills. We have done nothing but purchase fried land since the wildfire hurricane twenty years ago! I'm going to create my very own wildfire hurricane right now!"

Al Sr cocked back his rifle and yelled, "I mean it! I will shoot you father! I can't risk burning down our ranch or our village like Baltimore city!"

William Jr gripped his lighter tight and flicked his thumb up~ (PAUSE) ~Kaboom! Al rang a shot, hitting his father right through his hand.

William Jr yelled, "Nooooo!"

His voice echoed through the valley like a train speeding through a tunnel. The gasoline went up in flames. William Jr's plan backfired. The fire department arrived at once, spraying the small forest of flames. The police weren't far behind. The County of Hollow Hills Police Department arrived on the scene a few seconds later with guns drawn.

Chapter3
"Sage; a Different Name for a Different Girl"

Mrs.Beckett loved the smell of sage and rosemary. She was a loving spirit who adored her husband, her herb garden and her unborn twins more than anything in the universe. She already named them after her two favorite herbs in the garden.

Mr.Beckett said, "Hey honey, come inside. Supper is ready. Bring some flavor with you."

She yelled, "Honey, come quick, something is terribly wrong!"

A short time later inside the hospital, the doctor said, "Mr.Beckett, please step over here, we need to talk."

Mr.Beckett replied, "Yes, doctor? Is everything okay?"

The doctor commented, "I'm sorry to give you this news. It looks like your wife will not make it; she's losing too much time"

Mr.Beckett screamed in a rage, "What do you mean?! She's my heart and soul!" The doctor whispered, "I'm sorry, sir." Mr.Beckett yelled again, "Noooo!"

He cried as the doctor grabbed his hand and looked him in his eyes and spoke of even worse news. The doctor said, "Your twins now have a thirty percent chance of making it through all this. We are doing our best, but it's out of our hands."

Mr.Beckett yelled again, "You can't take my family away from me!"

Both babies were born, but only one was crying as loud as a fire truck siren. Sadly, only one twin survived the harsh labor. Tragically Mrs.Beckett didn't make it either. Her name is Sage, a different kind of name for a different kind of girl.

At Eleven years old, Sage plucked grape tomatoes from the garden her mother once loved so dearly. Her dog Blue ran over to her, as she went inside the house. It was time for them to go feed poppa.

Mr.Beckett had fallen ill over the past few years. Sage took care of him, the house and Blue. She quietly sat at his bedside and made a budget for the bills as he ate. With little income, Sage figured out how she and her Poppa would survive.

Sage said, "Hey Poppa I'm getting ready to cook chicken, rice, peas and homemade biscuits for us again. Would you like some lemonade?"

Poppa coughed and smiled, "Hey Sage, you are something else. Just like your mom was. I love you. Some lemonade would be a delight my dear."

"I love you too," she replied.

They hugged so tight Blue jumped on the bed to get in on the big hug.

As she licked their faces, a broadcast came on the radio speaker, stating: (The wildfires are jumping over the mountains. Please evacuate! This has been an emergency broadcast system alert! I repeat the wildfires are jumping over the mountains. Please evacuate immediately! This has been an emergency broadcast system alert!) The radio cut off. Blue jumped off the bed, ran to the door and barked. Sage looked outside the window. She could see smoke pouring over the mountains like a smoke tsunami. The smoke was so dark she couldn't see the trees anymore. She knew it was time to go. She looked at Poppa in a panic.

"Poppa, it's too much fire!" Sage yelled.

"Poppa, we have to go now!," Sage yelled again.

Poppa cried out, "No, not me!"

Sage grabbed his arm and pulled him up on the bed, trying to get him into his wheelchair. She screamed, "Poppa, you're coming with me!"

He then looked her in the eyes with tears running down his face and his legs trembling. As he tried to stand frantically, he fell on the bed trying to get in the wheelchair and shouted, "I am only a burden, you can't drag me with you!"

Knowing that Poppa was right, Sage sobbed loudly "No!"

Poppa cried and yelled, "Listen, you have been strong your whole life. Don't stop now! You and Blue will have to head east. You will find shelter there, trust me. Head east!" Poppa spoke firmly, "My grandfather and father died in this house and so will I. I love you always, Sage; Now go!"

Sage jumped up, grabbed a few things, and ran off with Blue just in the nick of time. She turned and saw the fire burning everything around the house. It was going up in flames fast. She could hear Poppa yelling, "Find the Stanley ranch!"

With his last breath fading away like a distant music note. "To find the Stanley ranch, head for the Hills!"

Her name is Sage, a very different name for a unique type of child. Sage and Blue outran flames from The Big Blowup and her story began August,20/1910.

Chapter 4
"The County of Hollow Hills Inmate"

In the jailhouse an announcement broadcasted over the intercom, "Stanley, last call for Stanley, please report to the visiting area."

At a cold scratched table, Al Sr and his family wait for William Jr to enter the visiting area. Al Sr's children could not wait to tell their grandpa the good news. As soon as he entered the room, a guard was reading a newspaper with the headline: (The Great Fire of 1911) He stood up from a desk and stated the rules to William Jr.

Two seconds later, Albert Jr and Alberta ran over to hug their grandpa and screamed, "We have a surprise for you!"

Then they all shouted, "You have a new granddaughter!"

Wiliam Jr looked at Mrs.Albert Stanley and asked, "Where's the baby? I didn't know you were carrying another bundle of joy?"

She replied, "No, look behind you William Jr, that's Sage, she's twelve. She was the only surviving member of her family after last year's wildfire season. We adopted her after hearing her horrific story."

Al Sr brought her over to meet his father. She began explaining her remarkable ideas about how she could rejuvenate the land with the gardening skills she learned from her father. Then Al's son Albert Jr explained his new hi-tech invention. The hi-tech sprinkler system that keeps the acres damp during any wildfire season.

Al's daughter, Alberta, said, "Grandpa, I have a great idea too. Instead of buying more cattle, we could build homes for families that have nowhere to go.

Anyone who survived a wildfire should have access to our land that can't be revitalized."

Al's wife nodded her head and said, "All the children are onto something. It will bring the family business more income than we could ever imagine."

William Jr said, "Is this true children?"

Sage hugged William Jr and said, "Al Jr, Alberta and I may be young, but we know how to keep the family legacy alive."

Sage kissed William Jr and said, "I'm a Stanley now."

The guard came over to the table and told William Jr, "Time is up inmate."

Later that evening, back at the Stanley ranch, Sage was tossing, turning and yelling, "Fire! Fire! Fire!"

So, instinctively Al Sr came running up to her room with a fire extinguisher. He found her having a nightmare. He quickly consoled her. Sage woke up and cried in Al Sr's arms. As he comforted her, he came up with an idea. Al tucked Sage in. When he walked out of the room. She jumped up and looked out the window. She became startled as if she could see a wildfire coming. Sage bounced back in bed as Al Sr returned and put a glass of water on the windowsill.

Al Sr went back to her room and kissed her goodnight again.

He said, "Lay down, try to get some sleep. Stay in bed. This water will extinguish any fire in your dreams. It will always be here for you I promise."

Chapter 5
"Furious Family Feud"

Decades ago, during the early 1870's, many years after the Emancipation Proclamation was signed by the Sixteenth President of the United States of America, Hollow Hills became a well established village in the clouds. After the Civil War, hundreds of Aboriginal Americans with copper skin Indian complexions fled back to Grandmother land, now known as the County of Hollow Hills. Their skin sparkled from riverbed reflections whenever the sun shined from a northern direction.

Two of the original county's founders, also leaders of the Aboriginal native tribes William Stanley Sr and Mr.Wilkens had a terrible falling out, which resulted in the first family feud of its kind.

They were in a competition to increase profits. These extra profits would purchase the untouched acres in between their properties. The extra space would make either the Stanley ranch or the Wilkens farm a greater source of revenue for their families.

It all started as a harmless joke. They both put snakes in each other's mailboxes and terrorized each other's livestock with cowbells and horns. It got bad when both of them spread nasty rumors about each other down at the town market. They tried anything to slow down each other's production, decrease revenue and torment each other's families.

The family feud continued for years, till one day the for sale sign on the vacant lot read sold. The two men were very disappointed in themselves for not cooperating. They should've shared the cost a long time ago, but It was too late; They knew they could've bought the land together.

To their surprise, an immigrant Irish family began moving in. Fresh off the boat, the O'Connor's left the ongoing struggles of The Great Famine behind. After twenty-two years of struggling, they finally got a chance to start a new Irish potato farm in America. William Stanley Sr and Mr.Wilkens knew they had to stop the feud and team up to compete against their new dividing neighbors.

The Irish family flooded the markets with tiny Irish potatoes. This decreased William Stanley Sr and Mr.Wilkens profits. Not to mention the Irish business was a constant racket. Bright lights shined as trucks came in and out of the dark sheds. The foreign potato pesticides residue blew into the Stanley ranch and Wilkens farm. When the livestock got sick, William Stanley Sr and Mr.Wilkens decided to put a stop to this as soon as possible. It became such a great deal of disturbance and disruption, the two men immediately concocted a devious plan.

The next night, as soon as the bright lights faded out, they mixed up concoctions and loaded up their power wash trucks with poison and connected the hoses to the foreign Irish pesticide system. The entire potato farm became poisoned. No one understood why everyone who ate the Irish potatoes got sick. Soon it got linked back to the Irish potato farm. The town market filed a class-action lawsuit and the Irish family lost everything they had. Their only choice was to pack up and move back to Ireland. The dividing neighbors were finally out of the way. At least that's what Stanley Sr and Mr. Wilkens thought.

Not long thereafter, Mr.Stanley got a letter hand delivered to him as he sat on the front porch thinking about all his new opportunities. The letter was covered in clovers all the way from Ireland.

It read: I figured out it was you and Wilkens. Your families will pay for what you've done to my family. I'm Irish, it's in my blood to fight!

That didn't stop Mr.Stanley from taking out a loan to buy the contaminated Irish potato farm. Now that it was cheaper at a foreclosure price. It was almost a freebie.

Even though he could not raise cattle on contaminated land, he had a better idea to build a mansion on it. It would keep the tools and equipment operations running more efficiently and he could rent out storage space to Mr.Wilkens. Both the Stanley ranch and Wilkens farm ended up with much more space. This was the beginning of several prosperous seasons to come.

Chapter 6
"Pure Prime Beef"

The Stanley ranch was a tremendous success in the years to come. With the help of the children's ingenious solutions, everything went well with distribution and several other improvements.

The year was 1916, The Great Matheson Fire mysteriously destroyed bustling communities. Flames burned in all directions destroying section after section. Strong tornado winds carried lava amber storms across the mountainside forest; because of this, there was a wildfire in every narrow wooded area just outside of the valley. The local fire chief had it half contained.

Just in case of higher winds, higher temperatures or a small human error, Albert Jr had his hi-tech irrigation sensor sprinkler systems in place. He invented, patented and sold this to nearby ranches and farms. The

Stanley ranch had survived twenty more years of wildfires, thanks to Al Jr's innovative sprinkler system.

Sage was a tremendous help with rejuvenating the land. Her organic herb and vegetable garden made a substantial amount of income for the family. Her rosemary was extra special. It was the talk of the town. Down at the market the locals called her herbs magical. The special garden was believed to have ancient healing powers. Sage extracted the ancient powers with the roots of her labor literally. This unique nourishment spread all across the Stanley ranch.

Alberta committed to woodworking to make her ideas come to life. She was in charge of a humongous project. Alberta was Al's daughter, it was in her blood to build. She focused on her dream of providing a new life for wildfire victims. Alberta's long hot days paid off. She laid her first foundation on the adjacent lot across from the Stanley mansion.

Meanwhile, Al Sr was still raising cattle just like his father and grandfather before him, but not just any cattle. He raised pure prime Stanley beef. He fed the cattle the best pasture and herbs in the valley thanks to Sage's herbs. It was pure fresh prime beef that was very popular throughout the town. The Stanley ranch could barely keep up with the demand for its pure prime meats. This was great; Al Sr didn't have to worry anymore. He would have more than enough profits to retire soon.

Al Sr had already forgiven his father William Jr the second he was released from the county jail. Al Sr moved his parents to a small cottage on the Wilkens farm he built near the old wooden tower. Everyone was happy the Stanley ranch was a great success.

One night, William Jr called Al Sr over to the cottage to share a secret. It was a letter from Ireland. They sat down with a cup of coffee.

Al Sr's Mother, Mrs.William Stanley Jr walked into the cupboard and grabbed sugar cubes and said, "Here you go. Off I go."

She stepped back in the kitchen for one second and passed Al Sr a spoon and said, "You will need to listen carefully, son."

William Jr pulled out a fragile letter that looked one-hundred years old. He told Al Sr, How his grandfather William Stanley Sr gave it to him when he was just a young boy.

"This envelope holds some very important information I must share with you," William Jr explained.

As soon as he began to read it out loud, an announcement came across the radio. (The latest threatening wildfire has been one-hundred percent contained and extinguished.

We allow no one outside until the smoke clears and air quality is much better. Please stay tuned for further instructions this has been an emergency broadcast system alert!)

At that very moment, you can hear distant voices cheering, yelling and shots from rifles going off. The valley had survived another wildfire threat.

William Jr declared, "Son, listen to me. I don't have many years left. I must explain this letter to you."

Al Sr did not listen; he was too excited to listen. He heard the splendid news on the radio and ran to celebrate with his children.

He stormed out the door headed towards Sage's house first. The coffee in one hand and a shirt covering his mouth with the other hand, he ran through the smokey air across the field.

William Jr yelled, "Son, get back here. I must read this letter to you!"

Back at Sage's place, Sage wasn't excited at all. She tried to lie down and get some sleep, but there were too many haunting thoughts in her head. She laid in the darkness for five seconds before dozing off. Al Sr reached her house and knocked, but there was no answer. He entered anyway.

Excited yet worried he yelled, "Sage, are you here? Are you ok?"

He headed towards the stairs and yelled, "Let's go celebrate! We survived another wildfire threat!"

Sage didn't reply, so he climbed the stairs. He approached her room, he heard sobbing.

Loud shouting came from the bedroom. "I shouldn't have left you, I should have stayed. I lost Blue! I'm so afraid"

Al Sr rushed to Sage, telling her, "Everything is ok. Wake up. You're having another nightmare, my dear," he said.

He hugged her and stated, "I love you, Sage."

Al Sr tucked her in and said, "This water you see here will extinguish any fire you dream of. It will always be here for you I promise."

Al Sr reached for the glass of water on the window seal then handed it to her. Sage took a sip and went to sleep.

Chapter 7
"Murphy O'Connor escape to the states"

After the family feud, Murphy and his family had no choice but to return to Ireland after going bankrupt and losing everything. Grandpa O'Connor accepted the loss and moved his family into an Irish workhouse. He gave up, but his son Murphy would not give up without a fight. He grew sick of the harsh labor and refused to settle as a slave.

Many years after the family feud was over, Murphy stowed away on a ship hiding out in the cargo area with the rodents. During his adventure across the sea, he survived by eating the exact rats he bunked with and some rations he brought along for his three month journey. He stretched every crumb, and slithered around the vessel like a snake in search of water every night.

Finally, twelve weeks had passed and he reached America. Murphy already planned how he was going to get to Hollow Hills. After a long journey across the country from hitchhiking, rail riding to the back of a mountain goat, Murphy finally reached the valley and the old wooden tower was in sight. He crawled like a ninja in the shadows of the moon. Murphy hid out in the tall corn fields as he waited for Mr.Wilkens to appear.

Early the next morning, the roosters were clucking at the morning sunrise. Murphy began to get ready for phase one of his devious plans to begin. Patiently, he watched Mr.Wilkens from afar, hiding in the cornfield for hours. Eventually, as Mr.Wilkens did his daily duties, he approached the corn stalks without a clue that this would be his last steps he ever took. In a split second Murphy snatched him out of sight without a sound and wrestled him down to the ground without a struggle. He did more than tarnish the Wilkens family name; he did some deadly, devastating damage that Mr.Wilkens would never live to tell.

In the end, Murphy O'Connor left Mr.Wilkens covered in clovers for all to see. Murphy had his family in Ireland he had to get back to. He began planning phase two, as he made his way back out of the states to Ireland. He returned and began training for phase two right away. With Mr.Wilkens out of the way, the focus was on the Stanley's now. Murphy craved revenge like a child desired candy on holidays.

Chapter 8
"Malcolm Grace & Nathan"

Malcolm always loved horses. When he was just a child, he dreamed of owning as many horses as he could care for. He dreamed of buying a huge horse ranch. One day, he met the love of his life, a beautiful cowgirl named Grace. Malcolm knew she was the one for him. Grace shared the same desire for horses as he did. She was tough as nails. Grace could ride a horse bareback. She enjoyed hanging upside down and standing up on a horse without falling off.

Malcolm didn't waste any time. In 1899 he married Grace and bought a five acre ranch with twenty-five horses. Soon the newlyweds had a baby boy named Nathan. Nathan grew up with that same love for all beautiful animals that his parents had for horses.

When Nathan turned sixteen, all the nearby counties were advised to evacuate.

The sky started raining hot scorching lava in random places.

Malcolm said,"Natural disaster turned massacre from America to Africa. Let's pack it up!"

On that same birthday morning, their county was put on the evacuation list. There wasn't any time for a party or gifts. Grace and Malcolm have been preparing Nathan for something like this all his life. Malcolm taught him how to use different hunting weapons at a young age.

Malcolm always stressed the point of safety to him. He always told him only to use them if needed for food or protection. His mother, Grace, taught him to always expect the unexpected. Nathan was an intelligent, mature young man; he was mostly quiet and to himself, he always respected his mother and father.

They did a wonderful job raising their son to become a great young man. For fifteen years his parents have been preparing for this day. The wildfire season advisory had been coming across the radio for the past month. Wildfire season was always a threat, and they never took any chances. Grace knew it was coming sooner than later.

Malcolm asked, "Grace, are we all packed and ready?"

Grace answered, "Yes sweetheart, we are all ready to rock n roll."

Malcolm gave Grace a big hug and a kiss.

He whispered in her ear, "I love you."

Malcolm said, "Son, are you ready?"

Nathan replied, "Yes father. With you two as my parents I am ready for anything!" His mother and father both had a horse. They were loaded with all the supplies they needed to survive such as food, water, tents, clothing, first aid kits, rifles and knives. Nathan was riding his own separate horse; all he had was the clothes on his back, a hunting knife, a hunting rifle and canteens of water.

Malcolm told Nathan, "Say your last goodbyes to your animal friends now. We will head out in a couple of minutes."

Nathan began hugging his horses, stopped and just looked around knowing it might be his last time seeing his animals. Grace and Malcolm were all set. The animals were running away. The family hopped on their favorite horses and led the way for all the horses and other animals to follow. Leaving hit Nathan like a ton of bricks, but he kept his composure and he knew where the family was headed.

Malcolm yelled, "To the Wilkens farm we go!"

Malcolm's old friend Mr.Wilkens was a great friend to the family. He had a nice farm on a mountaintop hidden in the clouds. They haven't seen Mr.Wilkens in years, but now was the perfect time for a visit. Down the old winding trails up the mountainside, the horses led the way until Malcolm and Grace brought their carriages to a stop for a quick readjustment. Nathan's horse panicked and kept moving forward up the forest on the mountain side. Nathan calmed him down, he stopped and they rested for a water break. Nathan looked back for his parents as smoke appeared in the sky slowly covering his view down the mountain. Grace's horse ran off as smoke appeared more heavily.

Nathan yelled, "Mother!"

Malcolm grabbed Grace and helped her onto his horse. They saw Nathan in the distance but the smoke in between them was getting thicker and thicker.

Grace yelled back, "Head east, son, just keep going east!"

He did what his mother said and followed the winding trail all the way east gradually up the mountainside. Malcolm's horse came to a rushing halt. Grace fell off, Malcolm jumped off to help her from the fall and his horse ran away. They were stuck running as fast as they could. Somehow they got separated in the smoke. The wildfire intensified. Grace fell down to the ground as the flames became visible, getting closer and closer to her.

Malcolm shouted her name in fear, "Grace! Grace! Grace!"

He stopped and crawled around feeling for her as he ducked under heavy smoky clouds.

Luckily, he grabbed her foot as the smoke covered the sky black. The flames circled them and closed in on them like a group of ferocious hyenas fighting over a small kill. He hugged her in the smoky darkness.

Grace coughed up her last uttering words, "Head east son! East!"

Malcolm squeezed her tighter and whispered to her, "At least Nathan is safe."

The wildfire spreads! Distant flames are accompanied by a funnel cloud rising to the opening sky…..

Nathan approached the Wilkens farm operated by the Stanley family. He was greeted with open arms. Alberta offered him a room in the Stanley mansion and said, "I hope you're good with your hands, I could use your help tomorrow."

Chapter 9
"The Late 1920's Irish meeting"

Back in Ireland, Murphy O'Connor's children Kelly, Ryan and Doyle packed hunting rifles, ammunition and knives, along with other survival gear. Ryan and Doyle finished up stuffing suitcases and sat at a table and poured champagne.

Kelly joined them and said, "Our time has come. Father is ready for us to arrive in the states."

Everyone held up their wine glasses and toasted to their new journey to America.

"Revenge is sweet. I can taste it already. We must be prepared," Kelly said.

She untied her ponytail and let her beautiful red hair down. Kelly's astonishing looks hid her aggressiveness and leadership very well. No one had any idea how well skilled she was. You would have never guessed she was running things in the O'Connor family.

The telephone rang. Ring ring ring.

Kelly said, "Answer it Doyle."

Doyle said, "Good day."

Murphy quoted, "A man is easily fooled by beauty. The fire is in the eyes."

Doyle quickly passed the phone to Kelly. She spoke to her father in code. Kelly said, "I've been training for this my entire lifetime. We can't waste anymore time. Everything my grandfather was robbed of after his struggle to save our family bloodline during The Great Famine years, it's the Stanley's and Wilkens's fault I had to grow up in impoverished Ireland, survive three Bloody Sunday's and the Irish Civil War! All the hard times in the workhouses our family had to endure for the O'Connor bloodline's survival. Finally, they will pay!"

Murphy replied, "You sure know our history well. Everything is set up. I will see you guys soon. I Love you Kelly."

She said, "I love you" and hung up the phone.

"We leave in twenty minutes. Father is waiting in the states for us to arrive."

Ryan and Doyle stood with their champagne glasses in hand. Kelly poured more champagne and they made one last toast to the demise of their family's old enemies.

"We will bring the Stanley's the biggest wildfire they have ever seen before and burn everything in sight. Maybe even burn the entire village down like The Tulsa Massacre in 1921," Kelley said.

They all yelled, "One, two, three O'Connor!"

Kelly's eyes lit up in rage like a five alarm blaze. She tied her beautiful red hair back into a ponytail. She walked toward the door grabbing her bags and hand signaled her brothers to exit.

"They say revenge is a dish best served cold, but in this case, it will be served on fire! Wildfire!" Ryan yelled.

Chapter 10
"Phase Two Irish Revenge"

The Great depression was no threat for Hollow Hills. The mountaintop village was well ahead of its time. It was a normal summer evening in 1929. The Stanley's just had dinner in one of the newly built homes, Alberta and Nathan completed. After dessert, everyone headed back to their home for a goodnight's sleep. Everything was great and going as planned. Al Sr was lying in bed with his wife sound asleep, only to be awakened by three Irish men pointing rifles at them.

Frantically, Al Sr screamed, "Hold on! Hold on! What do you want?"

He looked around the room and said, "Listen, you can have whatever you want, there's no need for guns!"

His wife woke up startled. She looked at her husband.

She shouted, "Please, put the guns down! There's no need for this! Take anything you want! You can have anything!"

Murphy asked, "Anything?"

"I just want revenge," he retorts.

Al Sr questioned, "Why?"

Murphy said, "You act like you don't know that your grandfather started this family feud? When he got my family, the O'Connor's, deported back to Ireland, I was only a small kid sent to work as a slave!"

The three Irish men stared at Mr.& Mrs. Stanley blankly.

Murphy asked Al Sr, "Did you see the letter my father sent your grandfather over fifty-five years ago?"

Al Sr replied, "I thought that crazy family feud was over well before I was born. Wait! You killed Wilkens, Didn't you? I remember I found him covered in clovers on my twelfth birthday Juneteenth of 1885."

Meanwhile, Kelly was on her mission to seek William Stanley Jr. Kelly began to put her hair in a ponytail, pulled out her make-up kit, and put two black lines underneath her eyes. She started to crouch down and crawl toward the cottage next to the old wooden tower.

Nathan heard a sound in the grass. His father taught him very well. Where he grew up, there was a sizable population of snakes. He could still hear his father, Malcolm's voice.

"Open your ears son, listen to this world, it always speaks to you. Survival of the fittest. You must always connect to the animal spirit inside of you, son. They all make noises but you gotta listen out for the sneaky snakes in the grass," Malcolm's voice said.

Back at Sage's house, she looked around in her dark bedroom as she sat up in bed sipping a glass of water. Sage eventually went back to sleep and dreamed that she felt heat, and smelled smoke. Suddenly a burst of fire spreaded all around her dream.

With her eyes tightly closed, Sage screamed, "Poppa! Poppa! Where are you?"

Sage began to search the burning house in her bad dream. She ran down the stairs, back up the stairs.

She shouted, "Poppa come on we have to go!"

She continued to have a terrible nightmare, tossing and turning in bed with her feet moving in a running motion.

Her Poppa said, "Slow down, I'm right here baby girl"

Sage never opened her eyes, but saw her father's face floating above her bed.

Her Poppa spoke, "I'm so proud of you Sage. You made it out of that horrific wildfire. You're all grown up, successful and so beautiful. You are so strong, don't be afraid. I'm in a better place. Now wake up!"

Sage cried as she replied, "I get my strength from you. I miss you, Poppa!"

Her Poppa spoke again before he faded away completely.

He said "I miss you my princess, but I'm here to warn you, the wildfire spreads, but it's no ordinary one!"

Poppa's voice faded, his final words were, "Wake up Sage! Wake up now."

She cried as she replied, "But I don't want to get up, Poppa. Even with the fire spreading, I just want to be here with you."

Sage frantically woke up, sweating and panting. She looked up at the ceiling, took a deep breath, and got out of the bed. She went to the windowsill and found her special glass of water. As she picked up the glass to take a sip, her eye caught an unfamiliar vehicle at the gate's entrance. She dropped the glass and immediately called Al Jr on the phone.

At the cottage Nathan heard a snake in the grass. He quietly grabbed his hunting rifle, then nonchalantly peeked out the window. Kelly arose from the grass and bolted to the cottage. She Put her back against the wall and got distracted by the lights coming on at the mansion.

To herself Kelly said, "It's time."

Boom! Kelly kicked in the door and immediately started heading towards the bedroom. Nathan jumped out his bedroom window, ran around the front of the cottage, then came through the front door Kelly just kicked in. He silently followed her in her own shadows.

Sage, Al Jr and Alberta ran to the Mansion with rifles in hand. They noticed the door wide open. Before they entered the mansion

Sage said, "Take off your boots."

They all nodded in agreement, and proceeded slowly, checking room by room for intruders. They could hear their mother & father begging for mercy. They crept upstairs to the master suite.

Back at the cottage, Kelly entered the bedroom. She woke up William Jr.

Kelly yelled, "They say revenge is best served cold but the O'Connor's are bringing an Irish wildfire hail storm".

Pow!!! A shot rang off. It hit Kelly in the back. She dropped her rifle and fell to the floor.

Everyone heard the shot go off. Accidentally Alberta shot Doyle through the bedroom door. Murphy and Ryan then shot at Al Sr, but missed. During all the commotion, Al Jr and Sage shot Ryan and Murphy Simultaneously. Alberta quickly ran to her mother, while Sage and Al Jr called the police.

Rapidly, William Jr and Nathan ran to the mansion. As they entered the mansion , they noticed two people sitting in the dining hall.

William Jr waved his rifle and asked, "Who are you on my land, in the house my father built."

The two strangers put their hands up and said, "Grace and Malcolm. Don't shoot please!"

Nathan fainted and fell to the floor. The authorities rush the house, bringing all the Irish out. Giant balls of clovers blew across the field and off the cliff, tumbling down the mountainside. No Irish men survived.

William Jr points to the cottage. Everyone ran over to check it out.

Nathan shouted, "She was right there, her rifle was too!"

Later that evening, the entire family sat down to eat dinner. Malcolm and Grace thanked the Stanley's for taking care of Nathan, when he arrived at the Stanley ranch.

Al Sr spoke. He said, "We survived the strangest wildfire ever. It started burning over seventy five years ago. Traveling over four-thousand miles from Ireland to Hollow Hills!"

William Jr pulled a letter out from under the table and began reading it out loud.

Grace interrupted him saying, "I have a surprise for you Sage!"

She handed Sage a picture of her Poppa and Blue.

"Malcolm found it under a pile of rubbish in the forest way back west," Grace said.

Sage clutched Grace as she kissed the picture.

Nathan was still in shock as he asked his parents, "How did you two survive that terrible wildfire?"

Malcolm answered with a question, "Do you believe in Natural Disasters?"

Nathan replies, "Yes."

Malcolm told the tale of a Tornado that came down from the heavens. He explained how it picked them up out of the burning circle of flames just in time.

Meanwhile, Kelly started a small fire just outside the Stanley mansion and disappeared into the forest. Al Sr smelled smoke and headed out to take a look. His father William Jr joined him and noticed a clover trail leading into the forest. They saw the small brush fire that just started adjacent to the mansion. Father and son quickly extinguished it.

William Jr said, "She must still be out there!"

They headed back inside. Alberta turned on the television. A tornado warning broadcast appeared on the screen.

The anchorman said, "A Tornado warning for The County of Hollow Hills will be effective until 6-19-1929 12am eastern standard time. Stay tuned for Volume II."

6-19-2021
Da Kozmoz Publishing
Happy Juneteenth Mom!
Happy Fathers Day Pops!
I Love You Kool Cuzz